Fitzhenry & Whiteside

Paperback 2003 Fitzhenry & Whiteside

Fitzhenry & Whiteside Limited
195 Allstate Parkway
Markham, Ontario   L3R 4T8

In the United States:
121 Harvard Avenue, Suite 2
Allston, Massachusetts 02134

www.fitzhenry.ca   godwit@fitzhenry.ca

*Fitzhenry & Whiteside acknowledges with thanks the Canada Council for the Arts, the
Government of Canada through its Book Publishing Industry Development Program,
and the Ontario Arts Council for their support of our publishing program.*

National Library of Canada Cataloguing in Publication

Gillmor, Don
The Christmas orange / Don Gillmor, Marie-Louise Gay.

ISBN 1-55005-075-3

I. Gay, Marie-Louise.   II. Title.

PS8563.I59C47 2003   jC813'.54   C2003-902554-3
PZ7

U.S. Publisher Cataloging-in-Publication Data
(Library of Congress Standards)

Gillmor, Don.
The Christmas orange / Don Gillmor / Marie-Louise Gay. —1st ed.

[32] p. : col. ill. ; cm.

Originally published by: Toronto: Stoddart, 1998.
Summary: Anton's Christmas list was 16 pages long. On Christmas morning,
there was one thing under the tree. It was an orange. Anton was not pleased.
He and his lawyer decided to sue Santa Clause.
Everyone came. It was the trial of the century.

ISBN 0-7737-3100-8
ISBN 1-55005-075-3 (pbk.)

1. Christmas — Fiction — Juvenile literature. (1. Christmas — Fiction.) I. Gay, Marie-Louise.   II. Title.

[E] 21   PZ7.G555Ch 2003

Printed and bound in Hong Kong, China by Book Art Inc., Toronto

For Justine,
my Christmas Girl.
— D.G.

ANTON STINGLEY'S BIRTHDAY WAS
DECEMBER 25TH — CHRISTMAS DAY.
When he was very young, he thought
the whole town was celebrating his
birthday. He thought he was pretty
special. When he found out everyone
was really celebrating Christmas, he
didn't feel special at all.

So his parents bought him extra
extra presents each Christmas.

Anton had a round head and
more toys than anyone.

Before his sixth birthday, Anton went to see Santa Claus at the department store. "What do *you* want for Christmas, Anton?" Santa asked.

Anton took out a list sixteen pages long. "I want a rocket ship," he said, "bright red, filled with Popsicles. A swimming pool, a dog that can sing . . ."

"Well," said Santa, "That should keep me pretty busy."

"A gun that shoots apple juice, hockey skates, someone to do my homework . . ."

"That's a lot for one boy," Santa said.

"I'm still on the *first* page," Anton said. "I also need a spy watch that takes pictures, a fire truck, two hundred cookies . . ."

"*Thank*-you, Anton," he said. "Merry Christmas."

"I'll leave you the list," Anton said, stuffing it into Santa's pocket. "See you next week. There's parking on the street."

On Christmas Eve, Anton dreamed of presents. They danced in his head like sugarplums.

But when he woke up and went downstairs, there
was just one small present from Santa under the tree. Anton opened it.
Inside the small box was an orange. *An orange.*

There had to be some kind of mistake. Where was the guitar?
Where was the *car?* Maybe they didn't fit under the tree. He searched
the house. Nothing. He checked the garage. No sign. Maybe Santa had
the wrong address. He woke up the Blinketts next door and asked if they
had six hundred presents addressed to him. They didn't.

What was he going to do with an *orange?*

There was only one thing to do. Anton would sue Santa Claus.

He went to see a lawyer named Wiley Studpustle. He was the meanest lawyer in the world. He ate peas with a knife. He never slept. He had a pet spider named Pumpkin.

In Wiley's dark office there were books everywhere. A half-eaten peanut butter sandwich lay on the floor.

"What do you want?" Studpustle asked.

"I want to sue Santa Claus," Anton answered.

"I see," said Studpustle. "And . . . ah, who is this Santa Claus?"

Anton gasped. "*You don't know who Santa is? Everyone* knows Santa Claus."

"I work late most nights," Studpustle said. He stared at Anton with eyes the color of mud.

"You know, *Christmas*," Anton said. "Presents. Carols. Ho ho ho."

"He's not that annoying fat man in the red suit, is he?" Studpustle asked.

"*Yes, yes.* That's him. He brings presents to children all over the world."

"And what did he bring you?"

"Well, he brought me an orange."

"An orange," Wiley repeated. "I see."

"But he didn't bring me what I *wanted*," Anton said. "I wrote it down. Sixteen pages."

"You have this in *writing?*" Studpustle perked up.

Wiley looked through the list and made small clucking sounds with his tongue. "He didn't give you a magic carpet?" he asked Anton.

"No."

"Or a bicycle that turns into an airplane?"

"No."

"Or a chocolate mountain, twelve kittens, a fishing boat?"

"None of it."

"Well," said Wiley Studpustle. "We'll see Mr. Claus in court."

"You mean you'll take my case?" Anton asked.

"Ho ho ho," Wiley answered.

Judge Marion Oldengray looked around her courtroom. *The Daily Porridge* had called it "The Trial of the Century."

"Your Honor," Wiley Studpustle said, turning around to face the people, "like every child here, my client Anton Stingley had the expectation of presents from a Mr. S. Claus on Christmas morning. Mr. Claus failed to deliver. We are suing him for breach of promise and we are asking for damages of eleven million dollars."

The people in the court gasped.

Wiley adjusted his suspenders and said, "I would like to call Mr. Santa Claus to the stand, Your Honor."

The crowd fell silent.

Santa walked past Anton. His blue suit smelled of mothballs. He sat heavily in the witness box.

"Did my client give you a list of presents he wanted?" Wiley
Studpustle asked Santa.

"He did," Santa answered.

"And did you deliver *any* of these presents,
Mr. Claus?" Wiley asked. "Did you deliver *a single one?*"

"I brought him an orange," Santa said. The
crowd moaned.

"An orange," Wiley repeated. "No bike.
No car. No hockey tickets. An orange.
How thoughtful," he said meanly.

Wiley leaned close to Santa. "You are sometimes known as Father Christmas, aren't you?"

"Yes I am," Santa replied.

"And Kris Kringle, Père Noël, Jolly Old Saint Nick?"

"Yes, all those names."

"I would suggest to you," Wiley said, "that you are neither jolly nor a saint. And your name *isn't even Nick*." Wiley turned to the judge. "Would someone who is *innocent* need so many names?" he asked. "I think not."

Judge Oldengray banged her hammer three times. "Court is adjourned for lunch," she bellowed.

When Santa left the courtroom, reporters pressed around him. "Is it true, Mr. Claus," one asked, "that you brought yourself a brand new car this Christmas?"

"No," he sighed, "I drive a sleigh."

Questions filled the air:

"Hey Kringle, if that's your real name, how much money did you make last year?"

"Why don't you hire tall people?"

"Are your reindeer non-union?" And so on.

Santa's heart filled with sadness.

After lunch it was Santa's turn to ask questions. He called Wiley Studpustle to the stand.

"Mr. Studpustle," Santa began, "Did you always want to be a lawyer?"

"Always," Wiley said.

"There was never a moment when you wanted to become, say, a zookeeper?"

"Who wants to be a *zookeeper?*" Wiley sneered.

"I remember a little boy who wanted to be one," Santa said. "He loved animals. One Christmas, many years ago, I brought that boy a baby crocodile named Crunchy." Wiley began to sweat a bit. "And that boy's name," Santa said, pausing for effect, "was Wiley Studpustle."

The crowd gasped.

Wiley suddenly remembered Crunchy and his cute smile, and he began to weep. "Oh, Crunchy," he cried, the tears staining his dark suit. "Oh, my Crunchy-Bunchie." He buried his face in his hands and sobbed quietly.

Santa turned to face the people in the court. "You're unhappy that I didn't bring Anton Stingley what he wanted for Christmas," he said. "You're unhappy that I don't always bring you what *you* want. Well," he said. "It isn't my job to bring you what you want."

The crowd was shocked. They cried out in protest.

"My job," Santa said, "is to bring you what you need." He looked down at Anton. "How many toys do you own, Anton?" he asked.

"I don't know," Anton said meekly. "Twenty?"

"In fact, Anton," Santa said, "you own one thousand, one hundred and forty-one toys. Nine hundred of them have been played with exactly once. One hundred and twelve you haven't even touched. You didn't need six hundred new toys, toys that will sit unplayed with. What you needed was something precious and small. You needed one perfect, mysterious orange."

The people in the court looked at Anton.

"For hundreds of years I've been doing this job," Santa said. "I've survived blizzards and budget cuts. I've had reindeer problems."

"And now you're unhappy," Santa said heavily, looking at the people. "Well, I'm unhappy too. I quit."

A silence descended on the courtroom. A silence so big, so . . . *silent*, that you could hear a mouse breathe. Santa began to leave the courtroom.

"You can't quit!" someone yelled. "You're *Santa Claus*."

"I bring each of you a present every year," Santa said. "When was the last time any of you gave *me* a present?"

Santa walked out the door and started down the courthouse steps. A murmur moved through the crowd, a murmur that became a hum that grew into a buzz. What had Anton done?

What had *they* done?

Out on the street, Santa put his hand up to
hail a taxi. Anton knew he had to do something.
"*Santa!*" he yelled. "*Wait! Wait!*"

A taxi pulled up and the door opened. Anton raced down
the stairs. He didn't know what he was going to say. He wanted to say that
he was sorry he had taken Santa to court. That he knew he had enough
toys. He didn't want to be naughty. He wanted to be nice. What do nice
people *do*? he wondered.

They did nice things. Anton wanted to give Santa a present. But what? In his pocket he felt something round. Something mysterious. He took it out and looked at it. It was an orange. It was as round as Anton's head and as perfect as the sun.

It was the Christmas orange.

Anton held it up to Santa. "It's for you," Anton said. "Merry Christmas, Santa."

The crowd stood on the courthouse steps, holding its breath.

"Where you going, buddy?" the cab driver asked Santa Claus.

Santa took the orange and smiled. "I'm going to the North Pole," he told the cab driver.

"I'm going back to work."